# Vikings: The Bigfoot Saga
## By
## Gayne C. Young

I greatly appreciate you taking the time to read my work. Please consider leaving a review wherever you bought the book or telling your friends about my book to help spread the word. Visit me at my website www.gaynecyoung.com. While there, subscribe to receive free bonus chapters and photos, information on upcoming projects, and news.

Follow me on Facebook at
https://www.facebook.com/authorGayneYoung

For Larry Weishuhn and Tim McCreary who look like

Vikings.  Well, older Vikings.

I am Agnar Vray, son of Bothvar, son of Einar.

Sagas of my skills in battle are told round fires and in halls on all known lands.

With spear, axe, and sword I have no equal and though I lie dying on the field of battle, I prepare to enter Valhalla having never been bested in combat.

By man.

*tveir*

The horse fight was the first of the afternoon's celebratory activities.

Two Beothuk slaves led a mare heavy in estrous into the log walled arena and tied her to the center pole. The mare shook in frenzy at the noise from the crowd and her agitation in turn rallied the gathering of warriors and artisans, workers, farmers, and slaves to even more energetic yells and chaos. A young warrior named Thrain led a pitch colored stallion into the arena and the horse frothed and chomped at the bit from the smell of the mare and from the fervor of the crowd. Opposite, Rognvald and his son Kotkell led a stallion of rust color into the arena. It too bucked at the smell of a potential mate and at the crowd and at the other stallion. The men did their best to restrain the horses then looked to the decking above the arena for instruction. Beigarth sat heavy with wine and hubris at the day's proceedings. It had been four years since he and his brother Angar had made their way to Vinland at the urging of their cousin Leif and today was the beginning of a week of

6

celebration of the colony's success. Despite finding a land thick with timber and fur, an abundance of fertile soil, and a sea weighed with fish and seal, the first two years had been difficult. Nothing came easy. It took more than a month to secure labor in the form of ninety-eight Beothuk slaves. Once captured, though, they proved easy to break.

Almost too easy.

A dozen died from disease within a week of their capture. Two of the women killed themselves through sheer will after being repeatedly rutted and another three killed their infants at birth. They were a weak people, small and scrawny. They were good at fishing and sealing, however, and that first year was paid for with the meat, fur, and bone of those commodities. After a year of servitude, the Beothuk seemed to understand the reason for their existence as a people and their work efforts improved greatly. The second year they helped fell and trim into lumber over two hundred trees. A great longhouse was built as were boats to carry this third source of income back to Iceland. Angar led that trip and he returned the following year with more seed plants, livestock, and a dozen more colonists. The third year saw crops and animals flourish. Vineyards took to the newly deforested hills like weeds and Beigarth and his men filled vat after vat with wine.

Beigarth drained his horn of such and motioned to his wife Asta seated at his side for more. She raised her hand and a young Beothuk girl named Oubee rushed to fill Beigarth's horn. Folkmar pushed his horn forward and she filled his as well.

"Why have they all painted themselves this way?" Beigarth asked running his eyes over Oubee's half clothed body. "They look to be covered from head to toe in blood."

"You allowed it, Beigarth," Asta reminded. "It's some sort of spring celebration."

Folkmar drank and said, "They do it with red ochre. Damned if it doesn't set to the body like paint."

Folkmar stood and pulled his shirt up and his pants down to show the color covering the area circling his sex. "Took one from behind this morning. Tried washing it off twice - nothing.  My cock will look like a bullseye for some time!"

Beigarth bent over in laughter and Asta rolled her eyes and told her husband she'd rather watch the horses fight than see the visual proof of Folkmar's coupling. Beigarth laughed through his amusement then stood. He raised his hand and dropped it sharply and the stallions were released.  The horses charged one another and the arena was filled with the sound of thundering hooves followed by the impact of 1,500 pounds of muscle colliding. The black came up under the rust colored challenger and pushed him back and over. The black reared and brought his hooves down making splinters of the rust's teeth.

The rust lunged upwards and caught the black's forward haunch with broken teeth and came away with a mouth full of blood and cut flesh. The black withdrew in pain and the rust stood in challenge.  The stallions launched at one another and their legs intertwined in midair, becoming one in combat.  The black bit into the rust's neck and the rust swung his head into the black and grounded it. The rust brought its hooves down hard and the black's eye socket crunched beneath the weight. The rust reared back and the second drive of its hooves turned the black's eye to pulp. The black fought to stand but the rust came down again with shattered teeth and this time took away the black's ear.

"Should you pay me now?" Beigarth chided Folkmar.

Folkmar raised his voice over the screaming of the crowd and offered, "Double or nothing!"

The black fought to stand but the rust pushed it against the wall and pummeled it with thrashing hooves. One of the downward cuts sent the rust's hooves through the black's muzzle and part of its nose and lip were severed. The rust raised once more and came down against the black's skull with the sound of collapsing bone so loud that even over the fervor of the crowd, all knew the fight was over. The two Beothuk slaves returned to the arena and quickly led the mare from the ring and the rust colored stallion followed.

Beigarth stood to applaud the fight and when he sat Folkmar was stewing at having lost the bet and motioning for more wine. Asta watched as the fallen stallion was dragged from the arena by ox and painted Beothuk. "I do like horseflesh," she reminded her husband. "Have them save the ribs for me."

Beigarth grunted in the affirmative and held his hand to Folkmar and said, "Now? Or shall we keep the wager going for the duration of the week's events?"

Folkmar drained his newly filled horn and replied, "Doubt we'll remember anything past this evening!"

The men laughed and slapped each other's back again and again until Asta questioned, "What in the name of the Gods is that?"

Four strong farmers carried a wooden cage to the center of the arena. One of the men attached a rope to the gate and inside a barely visible beast howled and scrambled about with such force that the cage appeared ready to give. Beigarth yelled to the man handling the rope, "Havard! What surprise do you have for us?"

"A surprise indeed my Lord," Havard yelled in return. He stepped to the edge of the arena and pulled the rope. The gate opened and the beast charged forward. It stood in the form of a man six feet tall, carved of sinew and covered in coarse pelage the color of midnight. It dropped to four legs then stood and roared through a muzzle of yellow canines. The colonists in the crowd exploded in cheer, questions, and wild musings. The Beothuk in attendance moaned in fright, waved their hands in warning while others shook in fear.

"What the Nidhoggr is that?!" Beigarth cursed.

Folkmar replied, "It look like the man son of a bear."

Oubee dropped the wine vessel and trembled in fear.

"Oubee!" Asta barked. "What's the matter child?"

"It's not a man. Or bear!" The Beothuk frantically stammered. "It's Aich-mud-yim!" Aich-mud-yim."

"Aich-muk?" Beigarth tried repeating. "Thought that was a bird."

"That's the auk!" Folkmar laughed.

Beigarth was embarrassed and retaliated against the young girl. "Speak Norse woman!"

"Oubee. Child," Asta tried. "What's Aich-mud-yim?"

"Aich-mud-yim. The Black Man." Oubee fumbled with the words. She tried again. "The Black Devil. The Black Devil."

"Black Devil?" Beigarth clarified.

"Yes. The Black Devil Bird," Folkmar guffawed. "The Aich-auk!"

"Black Devil. That's what all the reds call it," Rognvald declared. He and Kotkell entered the covered decking and sat. "We caught it in a bear trap just yesterday. The reds are scared shitless of it."

"You should to be scared," Oubee promised. "This is not a good thing."

"Shut your mouth!" Kotkell commanded. "And fetch me some wine."

Oubee did as she was told and returned with wine and horns for Rognvald and Kotkell.

"Names aside," Beigarth began anew. "What is that thing?"

"Some sort of animal," Rognvald answered. "One that wants to be a man. Shape wise anyway."

"Then let's watch it fight like one," Kotkell said pouring wine down his throat as fast as possible. "I've been waiting for this."

Rognvald looked for approval from Beigarth and once granted waved to Havard on the arena floor. Havard waved back and two elkhounds were released into the arena. The two dogs converged towards the beast in blurs of gray and silver. Their barks echoed from the arena and the colonists cheered them on with wild screams and the setting of bets. The beast lunged atop its cage and tried its best to climb the center pole but its claws could find no purchase. It dropped to all fours on the cage and screamed and swiped wildly at the baying dogs.

The dogs snapped their scissored jaws and jumped at the cornered animal. The beast lunged over the dogs and ran to the arena wall. It tried to climb the huge vertical logs but again its claws found no handhold. It turned as the dogs bore down on it. The beast dropped the lead with a downward blow to the

14

head.  The second dog jumped over the body of the first and sank its teeth into the beast's chest.  The beast screamed and ripped the dog from its chest by its back leg and swung its head against the arena wall with the clap of skull against wood.  It reared back and swung the dog into the wall again and this time blood and brain matter exploded onto the logs.  The beast hurled the smashed animal into the crowd with such force that it knocked the old lady it hit from her bench and over.

The colonists in the crowd were overcome with blood lust.  They howled in joyous appreciation.  The beast pulled the first dog from the arena floor and dragged it to the middle and swung its head against the center post repeatedly and with such force that its head came from its body and it flew across the arena.  The beast climbed atop its cage and beat its chest and roared in triumph over the cheering of the crowd.

"What the Gods is that thing?" Beigarth pondered in disbelief.  "Smashed the dogs to pulp."

Folkmar stood and killed his wine and pulled the shirt from his body.

"What's all that red skīta on your waist?" Kotkell asked.

Folkmar ignored him and offered Beigarth, "Double or nothing?"

Beigarth replied, "You're on, you crazy bastard. You're on."

"Seriously," Kotkell interrupted. "What is that red about your waist?"

Folkmar took wooden shield in hand and dropped from the decking into the arena. The crowd exploded in cheers and the chanting of, "Folkmar! Folkmar! Folkmar!"

The beast watched as Folkmar charged forward his shield held before him and screaming in challenge. The beast dropped to the ground and took the headless dog into his hands. He swung the cadaver into the shield. Blood splattered the shield and over Folkmar's head. The impact of the blow knocked him through the air ten feet and onto his back. Folkmar rattled his head and tried to stand but the beast was on him. It swung the dead canine like a club and Folkmar barely got his shield up in time. The dog exploded with blood and

16

intestines against the shield. Folkmar rolled over once more and tried to stand. The beast grabbed his leg and flipped him up and over onto the hard floor of the arena. Folkmar spun around and strafed his shield against the beast's shins. The animal yowled and drove its fist into and through Folkmar's shield. Folkmar rolled away and jumped to his feet. The beast drove forward and Folkmar jumped for a half piece of his shield and raised it but the beast made splinters of it as well. Folkmar ran towards the decking screaming, "The bets off! The bets off!"

Beigarth exploded into laughter and doubled over in an attempt to catch his breath. Rognvald pulled the axe from his side and threw it into the arena. Folkmar jumped up and caught it by the handle. He hit the ground, turned and swung. The iron blade caught the beast in the neck and its head was severed and the body fell in a cloud of arterial spray. Folkmar took the monster's head into his hands and held it high above his own.

The crowd went wild and the noise of its cheers carried far above the arena and into the woods high above it.

*þrír*

A sudden thunderstorm moved the festivities
from the arena and the grounds around it into the Great
Hall. The wooden structure was over 85 feet in length
and bowed in the center. At one end of the building
was a barn and in winter it held horses, cows, goats,
chickens, ducks, and auk. As it was spring, it was empty
but the smell of its seasonal residents remained and
mixed with those of smoke from the center fire, wine,
mead, cooking horse flesh, and the close quarters of
over a hundred people in various states of inebriation
and the raging blood lust and heavy sexual appetite that
come with such. People moved about in all manners of
dress. Some women were decked in their finest and
accentuated by eye makeup, broaches, and armbands of
silver, glass, gold and stone while others wore their daily
clothing of long underdress covered by a smock stained
with the work of farming, animal husbandry, child
rearing, and cooking. Men wore tunics of every color
yet some wore nothing but woolen pants and many had
tattoos upon their chests and arms and leather belts

affixed with axe, sword, or knife cinched tight about their waist. All of the Beothuk were painted red in celebration and some stood naked to the waist and others fully clothed and some wore jewelry made from things obtained in the woods or from dead animals or from goods discarded from the colonists. Oubee was more decorated than the other of her people. She wore a woolen skirt and a breastplate made of whalebone and her black hair was greased slick against her head with cod oil and adorned with twenty seal whiskers.

She stood transfixed, staring at the beast's head adorning a pike before Lord Beigarth's chair. All her life this thing before her had been just another tale that the elders told. The beast was mentioned in stories of creation and in the warnings of traveling far from home. The beast was a fable yet here it was, posted in death and displayed in pride.

Oubee was hypnotized by the head and scared of it even in death. She stared in fear at the beast's opaque eyes glazed over in the beginning of decay. She was drawn to this nightmare in a way she couldn't understand. She wanted to feel the black hair covering

20

its oddly tall crested head and to test how sharp its yellow canine teeth were with the tip of her finger.

"Still scared of this thing?"

Oubee jumped at Folkmar's sudden appearance.

"Don't think he can harm you none," Folkmar continued. "Lest his head can grow back his body."

Oubee lowered her chin and muttered that she knew not what Aich-mud-yim could do while living or while dead but that her people had known since the beginning to keep their distance from the Black Devils.

"Devils?" Folkmar slurred. "There's more than one?"

Oubee pulled the cloth from her belt and dipped it in wine. She dabbed at the cut above Folkmar's brow. "They are an old tribe. Since earth was new. This was the first I've ever seen. The first most has seen."

Folkmar took Oubee's gesturing hand in his and said, "One less now."

He looked Oubee up and down and his blood rose from the sight of her. Since capturing the first round of Beothuk those many years ago, Folkmar and his people had seen Oubee's kind as little more than a commodity. They were goats in the shape of men. They were weak, ate the vilest things, and lived in revolting conditions. Still, the females of the species could be enjoyable. Folkmar had taken many of the savages but had not been with Oubee.

Yet.

But looking at her in the dim light of the longhouse, after the thrill of killing the beast and a day of heavy drinking raised the idea of rutting her. Folkmar was just about to take her when Beigarth approached.

"Feel bad for killing him?" Beigarth slapped Folkmar upon the shoulder and drank. "Wonder what it would have done to you had Rognvald not thrown you an axe."

"Wonder no more my friend," Folkmar replied. "I would have ripped his head off."

Beigarth laughed. "Oubee, do you believe this man's boast or do you find it to be as big a load of goat shit as do I?"

Oubee smiled nervously at the question she knew she could not answer.

"I might get the chance to prove it to you yet," Folkmar declared. "Oubee says there are more out there. She says they're from an old tribe."

"You don't say," Beigarth countered.

"I don't know my Lord…I have never seen one…"

"No one should have seen this one," Beigarth reasoned. "Its parents should have killed it at birth."

Folkmar spit wine. "Parents? You think this thing…Was human?"

"Not human like us," Beigarth explained. He gestured to Oubee. "Like her people. I'm guessing it was a freak born of one of her kind. Albeit less evolved."

"Leave the girl alone," Asta said appearing next to her husband's side. "Food is ready."

Beigarth looked at Asta in question.

"You have to say something," Asta reminded.

Beigarth grunted and frowned. He killed his horn of wine and handed the empty vessel to Oubee. "Fill this," he said and moved to before his chair.

Oubee nodded and complied. Beigarth took the full horn of wine and drank.

"Friends," Beigarth boomed. The hall took its time but soon settled. "Six years past my cousin Leif, son of Erik, crossed the void to this new land and found an untapped source of wealth and prosperity. A year later, many of you gambled on this promise and joined me and my brother Angar on this most unsure of propositions. Today, in the spring of our fifth year I stand before you to say we have succeeded."

The hall erupted into cheers. Norsemen clapped their leader and the Beothuk echoed in obedience.

"So let us partake of all we've worked for," Beigarth encouraged. "Drink, eat, fight, love, rut, repeat! And repeat again!"

Drinking vessels were thrust upwards. Men and women cheered. Children screamed in contests to see who was the loudest and the Beothuk cheered in the language of their people. Plates towering with horse, mutton, venison, and seal were passed around. People gorged on cooked meat and drank like fish. Music blared and people danced. Games of chance were

24

played, fights were fought, and sexual appetites were entertained. The hall was in a state of pure hedonistic debauchery.

And then the main door exploded inward.

Lumber splintered and shards of wood shot through the air.

The hall stared in disbelief and eerie silence as eight feet of animal in the shape of a man filled the doorway. The beast ducked beneath the lentil and entered. Lightning flashed illuminating the dark figure as it entered the hall. The longhouse remained transfixed. All stood quiet, unable to break their trance on the unknown entity. Not even the sudden crack of thunder distracted the crowd. The beast stepped forward with a strong and deliberate gait. A Beothuk stood in its path. A violent swing of the beast's arm sent the man flying and into the distant wall. His neck snapped and he fell to the floor dead. The men of the hall pulled swords or axes and a few carefully reached for shield or spear and several women pulled knives. The beast roared and the force of its vocalization shook the hall. Three more beasts each matching the first in size and build answered the call by entering the hall. The building stood silent until Folkmar dared speak.

"Fuck me."

The four beasts tore into the hall destroying all in their path. One dropped to all fours and upended the front table and threw it into the crowd. Another grabbed a warrior in each of its massive hands and smashed their heads together and into a foam of splintered bone, hair, blood, and brain matter. A Norseman wielding an axe came at the third monster but was met with a sideway blow so strong it sent him flying and into a mother and nursing child. Kotkell sidestepped the fallen and came at the beast with a spear. The monster pulled the spear from Kotkell's grip and swung it into the warrior's ribs. Kotkell was knocked to the ground, holding shattered ribs and gasping for breath. The monster worked the spear like a club. It howled and swung at anything that moved.

The first beast drove through the crowd toward Beigarth's chair and the head displayed before it. Folkmar stood in its path with bow drawn. He loosed an arrow and the shaft pierced the air and embedded

26

into the monster's shoulder. The giant grunted in pain, pulled the arrow from its flesh and vaulted twenty feet through the air to land before Folkmar. It raised both arms and Folkmar charged forward and drove an arrow into the creature's abdomen. The monster's fist hammered downward and Folkmar rolled to the side and away from the strike. Beigarth appeared and swung his sword into the giant's forearm and into bone. Beigarth struggled to pull the blade from the beast. The monster pulled the sword from its arm and twisted it with such force that Beigarth's arm was wrung from his body. Beigarth fell to the ground grasping his wound. Folkmar drove his sword into the back of the animal's leg just as Asta came with knife in hand to protect her fallen husband. The monster roared in pain as Folkmar sunk his blade deeper into the animal. The monster turned and knocked the warrior from its leg with such force that Folkmar heard his own ribs crack. The beast turned back to the head of its kind upon the pike. It gingerly removed the decapitated piece and cradled it in the crook of its arm. Asta took advantage of this moment and drove her knife into the creature's chest.

The monster yowled and took Asta's head in his free hand and in one fluid motion ripped it from her body and plunged it onto the pike that once held the monster.

Beigarth's scream of loss was so loud it drowned out the ongoing destruction of his longhouse.

*fjórir*

Angar and his crew of thirty berserker warriors landed at the colony six days following the attack to find the docks deserted. At first they attributed the absence of a greeting to the inclement weather they had faced during their crossing from Iceland that had put them a week behind schedule but within minutes of standing on firm ground, Angar immediately sensed something was wrong. His men, weary from travel and heavy with lust for and the anticipation of Beothuk women, dismissed his worry. Chief among these was Angar's right-hand man Gunnar.

"You're just upset baby brother isn't here to meet you," Gunnar jested. "I tell ya', he and the rest are in the Great Hall, thanking the Gods for harvest by rutting, drinking, and fighting… And I look forward to joining them as soon as legs can carry me there."

Angar smiled and palmed the sword at his belt. "Aye, that is where I hope they be. But would we not hear the celebration from here?"

"Not all Norsemen rut with such loud cries as you!" a warrior named Kol offered.

Kol and Gunnar laughed and Angar grinned though still unsure of the situation at hand. He moved from his friends' joking and stared up the shore where the rocks gave way to the woods. Some one hundred yards beyond that lie the colony. Angar turned toward his men. "Varin, sound the horn. Let them know we've arrived."

Varin returned to the ship and retrieved his horn. He blew hard and the resulting blare shrieked across the water and up the shore. Angar nodded for another call and Varin responded with a louder and longer announcement.

The woods surrounding the colony came alive with the calls of crows and ravens and the sky grew black with their flight. Something was wrong. Angar pulled his sword and his men followed in action. Shields were handed out and when all were outfitted, Angar led them in two columns over the black rocks and to the road through the woods. The air beneath the overhanging trees was stale and the only sounds to be heard were the marching of men and the calls of soaring scavengers. At fifty yards from the colony, the wind shifted and the men caught the smell of rot and decay. At twenty-five yards from the colony they could hear the swarming of black flies and all knew something terrible lie ahead.

Angar motioned for Gunnar to take half the men through the woods to the far side of the colony. Once there, the two groups would merge on the village together. Angar watched the men head into the woods then turned his attention back toward the colony. Every door was shut, every light source covered, and the only signs of life was the pullulating of insects and a thin plume of smoke rifling upward from the Great Hall's main chimney.

Something was very wrong.

A distant birdcall told Angar that Gunnar and his men were in position. Angar moved his men outward and forward with hand gestures and the two groups converged on the village. They circled inward, carefully watching for men in wait or any other signs of trouble but found none.

The colony was a ghost town.

Angar and his men passed the outer houses and places of trade and made their way to the Great Hall. Two wolves stood at the main door scratching and licking the wooden planks before them. Varin raised his bow at the larger of the two but dropped his aim at Angar's instruction. Angar picked up a stone from the ground and threw it at the occupied carnivores. The wolves turned in Angar's direction and growled then retreated in a blur of speed. Angar and Gunnar rallied their men at the door. Gunnar and a warrior named Orn tried the door. "Barricaded," Orn whispered. Angar pushed on the entrance then stepped back and motioned for those with axes to open it by force. It took three hits before the interior was breached and when it did the smell of rot and decay, sickness and death exuding outward was overwhelming. The second axe man committed to the small breach and when he pulled his blade back two arrows flew through the opening and almost into Gunnar.

"Someone's home," Gunnar joked.

Angar walked to the axed opening and yelled, "Beigarth! It is Angar."

Angar's announcement was met with silence.

Angar yelled again, "Beigarth! It's Angar."

The faintest of whispers floated from the cut in the door. "Are they with you?"

Angar turned to Gunnar in question and then turned again and yelled into the hall, "I'm here with Gunnar and twenty-nine other warriors. Fellow countrymen. Open these doors."

From the other side of the door came the sound of latches and chains being undone, of wood being pried and of men groaning with effort. The doors opened inward releasing a wind so putrid that two of Angar's men heaved. Angar covered his face with his hands and entered the hall. He saw only darkness and smelled only death. When his eyes adjusted they focused on a site worse than battle. Dead were stacked like cord wood against a far wall. Sick lay covered in waste and filth upon the floor and women and children huddled in the corner balled in a group of fear. Folkmar walked from the interior, his hand held above his eyes to shield the light. "Angar," he wept. "Thank the Gods."

Angar hugged the broken man and instructed his men to fan out and open the doors.

"No!" Folkmar cried not letting go of Angar. "Don't. They'll come again. They'll come."

Angar pushed Folkmar from him. "Who will come? What transpired here?"

A voice from deep within the hall answered, "Evil."

Angar eased around Folkmar and toward the voice. He found Beigarth slumped in near death before his throne.

"Brother," Angar kneeled to embrace his kin but pulled back when he saw Beigarth wince in anticipation and noticed his missing limb.

"Evil," Beigarth repeated. "Evil is what transpired here. Evil…is what did this."

Angar called to Orn for water and it was brought and Beigarth drank feverishly.

"They did all this," Beigarth murmured from the brink of tears. Killed twenty… Killed my Asta. Ripped my arm from me like it was a twig."

"Who?" Angar asked. "Who did this?"

Oubee appeared from behind the throne. She stepped forward and sat next to Beigarth and wiped at his fevered brow. "Tell him," Beigarth winced.

"It was Aich-mud-yim."

Angar looked to his fallen brother for more information. None came.

"Who?" Angar asked.

Folkmar came to Angar's side. "What…is a better question."

"There were four," Beigarth murmured.

"Four men did this?" Angar asked in disbelief, gesturing at the carnage and destruction of the hall.

"Not men," Folkmar replied. "Something else."

Angar's face tightened. "There's no time for games or foolish puzzles, Folkmar."

"I wish it were," Folkmar continued. "They stood like men but were three, four…maybe five heads taller. Strong as iron. Covered in fur."

"What is this...this madness?" Gunnar questioned. He came to stand before Angar. He looked into Oubee's eyes and asked, "Girl, how long have you all been locked in here?"

"Six nights," Beigarth answered. He took a ball of cloth from his side and placed it in his lap and opened it to reveal the head of his wife. "Six nights since they took her from me."

Oubee reached for the severed head but Beigarth pulled back like a child harboring a toy. "No," he wept. "She stays with me."

"This is sickness," Angar exploded. He turned towards his men standing at the door. "Open this place. Burn the dead and wash the stench from here."

"No!" Beigarth cried. "No. They'll return! They'll come for us!"

"Let them," Angar fumed.

The hall was opened and the dead burned unceremoniously in a pit just outside of the village. The sick were bathed and attended to and put to recuperate in Rognvald's house. Women and children washed the walls of the hall free from blood and detritus and washed them again with lye soap in an effort to dissuade the hordes of black flies from returning.

Although running a high fever and suffering from the onslaught of gangrene, Beigarth refused to leave his throne citing he wanted his remaining days – or hours – to be at the last place he shared with his wife. A table was moved before the throne and there Angar, Gunnar, Folkmar, Rognvald, Kotkell, Havard, and a few others held council to discuss what happened and to make plans for the days to come.

"Tell us all your people know of these creatures," Angar asked Oubee.

"Are you entertaining this story? This delusion?" Gunnar interrupted. "These people went stir craze. Made sick with solitude and the surroundings of death."

"No," Folkmar assured. "Everything we've told you thus far is true."

Oubee fidgeted in thought and nervousness. Angar stayed focused on his inquiry. He instructed once more, "Tell us."

Oubee took a deep breath and shared the story she knew. She said that there are many stories but all began with creation. It was then that the Maker brought together all the animals in the woods. He found the bears to be the best that he had made. They were strong and very smart. He told the bears he would make two people from their kind. The Beothuk and the Aich-mud-yim. He gave the Aich-mud-yim all the bear's strength and little of its knowing. He gave the Beothuk all the bear's knowing but little of their strength. The two tribes went forth into the world. Each thrived and each suffered. The Aich-mud-yim found life hardest for their lack of knowledge kept them from comfort and ease. They knew not how to build, how to create, or how to improve their surroundings. For this reason they stayed in the woods always angry at the Beothuk.

Angar and the others listened intently, processing each detail to its fullest. A Beothuk servant girl named Demasduit brought them mead and all but Angar drank with heavy thirst.

"How deep in the woods?" Angar asked.

"The one we caught in our bear trap was two days in." Havard replied. "Thick country. Steep. Where the shore lands give way to hills."

"We do not go there," Oubee proclaimed. "It has been that way since long before me."

"Superstitions," Gunnar exhaled after a heavy pull of mead.

Angar ignored his friend and turned to Folkmar. "And their strength?" Angar asked.

"The first snapped elk hounds in the pit in half like brittle straw," Folkmar explained. "N' the blow it delivered to my shield was twice as hard as anything I've felt in battle." He paused to take a deep breath and held his ribs as he did. "And the one that did this was three times as strong as the first."

"So they can deliver the fight," Angar pondered. "How do they take it?"

"I put a blade and an arrow into one and it skipped merely a beat." Folkmar said.

"I sunk metal into that same one's bone," Beigarth said with heavy sorrow. "And it took my arm for the trouble."

"Did it bleed?" Orn asked.

Beigarth nodded and Folkmar said that it did.

"Then it can die," Orn said.

"How Angar?! Tell us how!" Kotkell stood from the table. "Because every man and woman here fought against those devils and the four of them killed twenty of us."

Rognvald put his hand to his son. Kotkell pushed it aside and continued.

"They injured ten and ..."

"Kotkell, know you place," Rognvald commanded.

"What makes you think you and your men can do any better?" Kotkell challenged.

Angar stood. "Because we'll not be surprised. Because we'll lie in wait for their return and because we crave vengeance. Now heed your father's advice and know your place."

Kotkell stood where he was. His father's hands appeared on him once more. He sloughed them off then sat having suffered the sting of humiliation.

"What is this bear tribe's name again?" Gunnar asked of Oubee.

"Aich-mud-yim."

"Have they returned since the attack?"

"No," Folkmar answered. "They've not appeared through the doors yet. But we've heard them moving through the colony at night."

"They howl. Cry," Oubee explained. "Like they are looking for something."

"Then tonight we'll give them something to find," Angar promised. "Tonight we take the fight to them."

Angar and his men and those from the colony
who were able prepared the main hall for battle. All but
the main door was closed to the outside. Doors and
windows were fortified. Smoke holes and chimneys
were barricaded and the interior fire pit set high with
wood and lit. The main doors were nailed open and
fires lit before them to show entrance into the hall.
Inside, men stood armed to the teeth and ready for
battle. Angar, Gunnar, and Folkmar stood at the doors
and watched as the sun eased below the forest. None
seemed bothered or nervous except Havard who paced
behind the others.

"Clear night," Gunnar offered. "Sól's brother
Máni will shine bright tonight for sure."

"Good," Folkmar stated. He put his hand to his
ribs and breathed hard.

"Will that be a problem?" Gunnar asked
gesturing to Folkmar's protective hand.

"Might keep me from rutting for a day or two
but not from a proper fight."

42

Gunnar laughed and Angar and Folkmar smirked.  Havard continued pacing.

"Havard," Angar began.  "What troubles you so? You move about like a rat on a troubled ship."

Havard settled in place and lowered his head in thought.  After a time, he raised his head then said to Angar, "I'm thinking this all be the fault of me."

"How so, friend?"  Angar asked with genuine concern.

"I brought that devil's spawn down from the mountains.  Had I not …"

"Had you not we would have met them eventually," Angar interrupted.  "The colony grows. We would have reached that timber in a year's time.  We would have faced them then."

"Aye," Havard replied.  "I just moved the calendar up.  And lives were lost because of it."

"We were caught off guard," Folkmar offered. "Surprised.  We were in the throes of celebration."

"True," Havard agreed.  His mood broke and he laughed and offered, "I was half way drunk."

"I was all the way drunk and my mind…"
Folkmar gestured to his head and to his crotch. "Both
of them were thinking of bending that red devil Oubee
over and splitting her up the middle."

"Normal everyday thinking then is what you're
saying," Gunnar joshed.

Folkmar nodded and said, "Of that you are
correct."

The men laughed and watched as the sky gave
way to soft blues and purples of a night illuminated by a
full moon. All but Angar took in mead and with each
drink grew heavy with anticipation and a readiness for
come what may. Angar instead stood motionless
watching from the entrance of the Great Hall for sign
of movement or threat. Oubee appeared next to him
and stared at the heavens above.

"Máni is not high enough," Oubee explained.
"In past nights, the Aich-mud-yim have not come until
later."

"You know the moon as Máni?" Angar asked.

"Yes. That is what your people have taught
me…"

44

"What do your people call it?"

"Kuis," Oubee replied.

"And what do your people say of the Aik Muds?"

Oubee smiled and corrected, "Aich-mud-yim."

"Aich-mud-yim," Angar repeated. "What do your people say of Aich-mud-yim?"

"That they are to be feared."

"Twenty lost tells me that your people are right."

"Their deaths are not a good thing to be correct about," Oubee admitted.

"No," Angar replied. "No, they are not."

The two stood in silence for some time. The fires outside the door burned down and Angar ordered them stoked. Gunnar and Orn stacked the fire with logs and headed back toward the door. They were halfway up the steps when a cry shriller than any they'd ever heard cut the night air. Gunnar and Orn turned round to face the village and Angar and his men moved to before the door. Angar turned to Oubee and she answered his unspoken question with a nod of her head. Angar replied with a nod of his own and gestured for her to move inside. She did and Angar and the others pulled their weapons and made ready.

The second cry was deeper than the first and it was echoed with a bloodcurdling howl. Gunnar turned to Angar then pointed to the origins of the sound, to before the hall and to its left. A moan of pain followed Gunnar's gestures and Angar pointed to its source at the hall's right. Gunnar nodded and held three fingers high. He dropped his hand as a howl carried from behind the hall. Gunnar raised four fingers and then pointed again at the cry's locations. Angar waved Oubee to his side and then whispered in her ear, "We count four. They circle us."

Oubee nodded and then whispered, "It is the same as nights before."

Angar nodded.

The air once more was cut by the unseen's screams. They circled the hall and cried to one another or to the night. Angar pulled one of two daggers from his belt. He passed it to Oubee and motioned her back inside the hall. The warriors all moved outwards from the hall's entrance and to the rear of the burning fires.

46

Angar banged his sword against his shield and the men followed in unison, the beat of metal on wood drumming faster and faster. Angar broke from the rhythm and thrust his sword above his head and screamed. Again the men followed and the night was shattered by the screams of some thirty Norsemen ready for battle. The cries ended and Angar challenged whatever the night held at bay, "I am Agnar Vray, son of Bothvar, son of Einar. Sagas of my skills in battle are told round fires and in halls on all known lands. With spear, axe, and sword I have no equal. And tonight you'll pay for your actions with your lives!"

Angar's claim was answered with banshee howls so loud the fire's flames jerked as if hit with a sudden gust of wind. Angar and his men stood ready, waiting for what the beasts' cries surely promised. Just inside the hall Oubee stood with her back against the wall, the dagger gripped tightly in her hand. Despite the cool night air she began to sweat. Her mouth went dry and her mind traveled through every nightmare she'd ever had in childhood. Her journey was interrupted by a feral shriek from the darkness before Angar and his men.

Gunnar whispered through gritted teeth, "It's moving away from us – outward."

"Cowards!" Angar barked for all to hear. He turned to Orn and ordered, "Torches!"

Orn and Folkmar ran to the hall where Oubee frantically gathered the implements called for. The two men bundled the torches in their arms and raced back to the fire. The staves were handed out and lit one after the other.

"Gunnar," Angar began. "The rear. Folkmar and Rognvald from the sides. Move forward. Kotkell, watch the hall."

All but Kotkell nodded in understanding and fanned out into the darkness. "I'm better than to watch," he complained.

Angar stared Kotkell into his assigned duty. He turned and led Kol and Thrain and four others toward the creatures' last call.

"Cowardice beasts," Kol grunted.

Angar ignored the comment and led his men forward and through the colony's vacant plaza. They passed the far side of the open expanse and to in-between two homes shut tight to the elements and to the calls of nights' past. The moon cast shadows of the homes made for a dark alley and the men held their torches high and forward to brighten their path. Their eyes had only to adjust to the sudden change when Angar spotted movement some thirty yards before him. Angar bellowed, "Fight me now and I promise Hel shall welcome you into her arms before the sun rises."

Angar ended his promise and threw his torch. The comet blazed forth and arched upward and fell at the distance illuminating a standing figure Angar and his men found hard to fathom.

"The Gods is th…"

Angar's query was cut short by a deafening roar. All men focused on the beast as it reared back in scream and beat its chest in dominance of its surroundings. Angar cast his shield aside and broke forward with sword ready. The creature dropped to all fours, turned, and charged into the black of night.

Angar returned to the hall boiling with rage and unspent adrenaline. His muscles strained and held tight like iron chain and his were eyes a portrait in fury. Gunnar and his men came from the darkness and soon they were joined by Folkmar and Rognvald and those who followed them. Angar looked to his men and saw in them the same choking of dark emotions and knew that their hunts were just as unsuccessful.

"We saw neither hide nor hair of the beast," Gunnar offered through rigid jaw. "But found tracks half the size of an elk's head. Like those of a man."

Angar broke his torch over his knee and tossed the halves into the closest flames.

"Of that size I have no doubt," Angar replied. "We saw it at a distance. A true jötnar."

"A jötnar?" Gunnar repeated. "A giant?"

Folkmar tossed his torch into the blaze and joined in the detailing. "A jötnar it was if it be same that hit us six nights past."

"We too found tracks. Jötnar made for sure. Spread wide and carrying elongated toes." Rognvald said. "Ours headed north."

"Into the mountains from whence they came," Havard said.

"But why return night after night and not attack?" Gunnar pondered aloud.

"They attacked only the one night is true," Folkmar agreed.

Angar's mind returned to Oubee and to the knowledge she possessed. He made his way past his men and entered the hall to see her and Demasduit tending Beigarth. The once great warrior was ashen and slumped before his chair. Oubee stood and met Angar half way. She lowered her head and said, "He has passed. I am sorry my …"

Angar eased Oubee aside and made his way to his brother's body. He took Beigarth's hand in his and whispered, "Go. Join Asta in Valhalla. Drink with Odin and share with him the sagas of your days. Sing of all you've done. Of wars fought and enemies slain and of the success of this colony. Worry not of this life, brother. But know that in it, I shall avenge you."

Angar stood and turned to the growing crowd of warriors come to see the fallen chieftain. "My brother makes his way for Valhalla."

All that stood before Angar nodded and cheered.

"Odin shall welcome him with open arms," Folkmar claimed.

Rognvald cheered, "Thor too shall be waiting. Ready to ask Beigarth how to fight!"

Angar's raised his voice above all the cheers and complements, "Yes. All this and more. We will celebrate his passing to the next life at dawn."

Beigarth was placed in a temporary grave as the sun rose from the sea. Despite most still full of worry and fear of the creatures the entire colony gathered for the event.

"His funeral will be in ten days time," Angar announced to the crowd.

A colonist named Allison and her daughter moved forward. "We shall sew him clothes for the journey."

Angar nodded in agreement and thanked Allison and her daughter with a short embrace.

"Oubee was his thrall," Kotkell decreed to Angar. "She should join him…"

"No," Angar declared. "Demasduit shall do so."

Kotkell's face strained in anger at once again being shamed by Angar.

"Oubee is needed in another capacity," Angar continued. "Demasduit will accompany my brother. Allison, see that Demasduit knows the importance of her duties."

Allison nodded and she and her daughter led Demasduit from the crowd.

"We all have duties to attend to," Falkmor announced. "Let us see to them."

The crowd began to dissipate but Kotkel stood where he was. He swallowed his anger, letting it fill his chest and moved before Angar. "What gives you the right to break our traditions…"

"Son!" Rognvald interrupted, making his way to Kotkel's side.

"Yes. It is best you collar your boy," Angar reiterated.

"Boy?" Kotkel spat. "I am a warrior, proven in battle and you'll treat me as such!"

Angar grew larger and more intimidating with every rage filled breath. He exhaled, "I have lost my brother," Angar declared. Our homes are under attack…"

"Angar. Please," Rognvald stammered. "Kotkel…He lost his fiancée in the attack. He…"

"He knows not his place!" Angar barked.

"I know my place and more of our ways far better than you…"

"I'll not stand here listening to a dream boy."

"Dream boy? I am a man and you'll do good to …"

Angar's fist went across Kotkel's jaw with the weight of an anvil. Kotkel collapsed backward and to the ground. Angar stood over him and commanded, "Dream, boy!"

All stood silent in reaction at Angar's blow except for Folkmar. He said, "Aye, is where a piece of shit should be. On the ground."

Angar moved from above the dream boy and took Oubee in his hand. "I shall stay at Beigarth's home this day. Get me food and prepare a bath."

Oubee did as she was told as quickly as possible. Within half an hour of Angar's instruction she had presented him with a plate of cold auk and squirrel meat and a heavy mug of mead. Of this Oubee apologized saying supplies had become limited in the days the colony had stayed in the Great Hall. Angar said it was of no fault of hers and devoured the meat hurriedly and carried his mug to the bath. There, Oubee washed him from head to toe with heavy lye and combed his hair with seal grease. Angar sensed Oubee's nervousness in performing these tasks and he asked what troubled her.

"I was Beigarth's thrall," she answered in a hushed voice. "Why am I not to join him in the afterlife?"

"Do you believe in our afterlife?" Angar asked. He put Oubee's hand to the back of his neck. She worked the muscles beneath the skin as she answered. "I have been told…"

"What you have been told isn't your way and it is right that you doubt it. But that is a matter for another time."

Oubee ran her hands to Angar's shoulders. They were rock solid and scored with raised scars that crisscrossed in every direction. "Then what will you have me do?"

"Why have these giants not attacked since that first night?"

"I do not know."

"What makes the night of their first appearance different than those since? Take me through that day. The day of the attack."

Oubee told of the celebration of the spring harvest. Of the horse fight and of the creature fighting in the pit. She told how it killed the dogs with ease and how it surely would have killed Folkmar had he not been given an axe. Oubee told of the sudden rain storm and how the festivities moved to inside the Great Hall.

"And then they attacked?" Angar asked. He leaned forward in the bath and Oubee brought her hands to his lower back. It too, like his shoulders, was a study in past cuts and lacerations.

"Yes," she answered.

"Why?"

"I do not know."

"Think. Who did they kill and why?"

"They killed those that were in their way. That fought…"

Angar turned in his bath. "In their way to what?"

The realization struck Oubee suddenly and she raised her voice for the first time in Angar's presence.

"The head," she exclaimed. "They came for the young one's head."

"And when they took it?"

"They left."

"So each night they returned…"

"They come looking for the rest of the young one's body."

"And where is that?"

"Beigarth ordered the meat cooked but it tasted so foul that it was given to the pigs. The hide was given to Hauk."

"The tanner. Leatherworker?"

"Yes. Beigarth told him to him to cure it for Asta."

Angar stood and Oubee wrapped him in a towel. "Then that's the bait we'll use to end this matter once and for all."

Hauk took great care in the skinning of the creature. After all, it was to be a gift to Asta. The colonist that gazed upon her wearing it as a stole or wrap would be taken aback at his skills. Yes, they would marvel at the fur for being from a monster but it would be his craftsmanship that they would be most impressed with and it was those skills that would bring him new business. Hauk had skinned the creature down the front, over its chest and down each arm and leg. He turned the fingers and toes inside out and fleshed the hide until it was free from muscle, fat, and membrane. He dried it then placed it beneath a pile of dry sawdust along with the hides of cow, pig, and deer.

This placement, Hauk told Angar, had been what had kept the creature's smell and whereabouts secret. Angar had Hauk remove the hide from the sawdust and clean it. Angar took the hide and cut slices into it to reveal whatever scent of the animal still remained. He then placed it high atop a pole between the fires before the Great Hall.

"The wind in the evening is off the sea," Folkmar said. "It will carry that devil's essence into the hills and into the noses of those jötnars."

"Then they'll come for it," Gunnar continued.

"And we'll be ready," Angar declared. He looked over his men and then to Hauk. "Tell them what you told me."

"Inside it's like any other animal," Hauk began. "Heart, lungs, and guts, all in their place and easily sliced."

"Its head came off harder than that of a man wearing mail," Folkmar declared.

"But you made it look easy," Rognvald laughed.

Folkmar guffawed and exclaimed, "Aye, I make all I do look easy because damn the Gods if I'm not but good at everything!"

Hauk dismissed the laughter and continued, "Folkmar is right. The creature's bones are stouter than any animal or man. And Asbjorn and I had a hard time quartering it for cooking. The bones are thicker."

"You should not have troubled so hard there, Hauk," Thrain said. "For it tasted like shit all the same."

"That's for sure what it smelled like when I skinned it," Hauk joked.

"Ripe as late summer afternoon gash, I bet," Folkmar joked.

The warriors all exploded into laughter and even Angar was overcome by the foul turn of words. He gave a hardy laugh then wiped the joyous tears from his eyes. He composed himself and began again. "Tonight, all will stay hidden in the hall but me. I shall wait here. Once the creatures enter the colony I'll bring," Angar paused to look upward at the hide oscillating in the wind, "This putrid remains into the hall. The beasts will follow. Thrain and Hauk will bolt the doors."

Thrain nodded at his job. Hauk swallowed the growing fear in his throat.

"Folkmar, Havard, Rognvald, and Gunnar, you shall shoot from the rafters."

"I'll have three arrows in mine before it can register the first," Folkmar promised.

"I hope so," Angar said. "Because I'll slice it in half before it registers the third."

The men cheered at Angar's declaration and fanned out among the hall to assure it was as secure as it was the night before. Angar watched the men then called Oubee to his side. "You are not needed here."

"Shall I help Allison and her daughter prepare Demasduit then?"

"No," Angar replied. "You have earned your rest."

Surprise washed over Oubee's face.

"Go to the house of my brother," Angar continued. "You may sleep there. In the bed if you like. I'll call for you if needed."

Oubee nodded and turned to leave. Angar stopped and turned her by her shoulder and looked at the belt cinched above her hips. He placed his hand at her waist then ran it over the dagger affixed to her belt.

"Good," he said. "Keep it close."

Oubee nodded and made her way to the home of Beigarth and Asta. She finished the mead that she had poured for Angar's bath then laid upon the bed. Nearly

62

a week of stress and lack of sleep crashed upon her and the weight of it all crushed her into the feathered mattress and into a deep, deep sleep. There, in the darkness of her subconscious, she saw the village of her youth. She was years younger and free from the understood shackles of her slavery. This younger version moved about friends and family, assisted her mother in adorning a dress with colored shells, and hugged her father when he presented her with a gift of seal whiskers. Oubee went further into the dream and became her younger self. She could smell the flowers around her sister's neck, feel the warmth of her father's hug, and taste the sweetness of berries just collected by her cousins. She was in a state of pure bliss, a happiness she had not felt in waking life for many years.

The feeling soon passed.

Darkness engulfed the village. Her family, friends, and fellow villagers turned to statues. Oubee opened her mouth to scream at the sight but only the slightest of whispers escaped. She watched this faint sound carry over those she loved and into the ever darkening forest. The trees parted and a hulking figure with pitch-black hair and yellow canines came forth. Aich-mud-yim took her whisper into his hands and crushed it. He moved forward and deliberately towards her. Oubee tried to move, tried to flee, to scream or even to die but was unable. She stood as stone until the beast was upon her. It pushed her back and down and then was on top of her. It drove toward the ground and forced himself inside her.

Fear tore at Oubee's insides and she fought to gain control of her muscles but she couldn't move. Couldn't fight the monster off of her. Couldn't free herself. Then she suddenly felt the dagger in her hands. She raised it and plunged it down into the giant's back. Aich-mud-yim screamed and reared back and off of Oubee. The beast contorted in pain, twisted and writhed then morphed into Angar. The monster's screams turned into Angar's laughter and he forced himself down on Oubee. She struggled and in the melee saw all her people in the same situation as her. All forced into the pain of forced intercourse by the Norsemen. Used, taken, and hurt by those from across the sea. The sight shook Oubee awake and she sat up in bed covered in sweat and trembling in fear. She fought to catch her breath and tried to calm herself. She was coming to terms with the attack being only a dream when she heard the monster roar across the colony.

Angar welcomed the monster's call and rejoiced in what he knew it would bring. He and his men were ready for the fight and eager to avenge the death of their loved ones. The first call was echoed by a second and then a third, each vocalization telling that the beasts were moving toward the Great Hall. Angar pulled the pike adorned with the creature's skin from the ground and waved it over his head, waved it back and forth in heavy succession allowing the dead beast's scent to carry as much as possible. The change in the dispersed was met with a call of rage. Angar scanned the darkness for sign of movement but saw none until the next scream cut the air. The four giants stood at the edge of the firelight. Angar dropped the pike, threw the hide over his shoulder and marched into the Great Hall.

The lead jötnar roared and beat its chest in challenge. The three that followed did the same and the night shook in a storm of animalistic cries and of heavy fists slapping taunt muscle. Angar entered the hall and made his way to its rear. He dropped the hide at his brother's throne and took his sword and shield in hand. The beasts lunged over the outer steps to the hall and into the doorway. They sniffed the air and recognizing the scent of their kin exploded towards it. Thrain and Hauk slammed the doors closed and braced them shut. Only one of the beasts turned to this action and when it did the rafters came alive and arrows rained downward. The lead jötnar took two arrows to the chest and at the impact of the second launched itself twenty feet into the air. The beast's two anvil fists splintered into the beam Havard stood upon. The impact knocked the archer backward and to the floor below. He landed on his back and the wind was knocked from his body. He struggled to breathe but had no time to do so. He notched an arrow and let it fly just as the beast landed at his feet. The arrow hit the monster just above the heart and it thundered in pain. It stepped forward and pinned Havard to the floor with a foot to the warrior's neck. Havard twisted his head and bit into the jötnar's foot. The giant pulled the three arrows from its chest and drove them down into Havard's face. In the rafters above, Folkmar took aim and sent his last arrow into and through the skull of Havard's killer. The beast fell forward and onto Havard in death. Folkmar leapt downward and onto the fallen beast and drove his sword into the spine just below the beast's head.

Thrain met the beast charging the door with a pike and the momentum of the two colliding drove the spear into and through the giant's lung. The jötnar struggled to pull the javelin from its chest but was met with a swing from Hauk's axe that took its arm off at the elbow. Thrain let go of his end of the pike and came at the beast with his sword. The beast fell at the blow and Hauk and Thrain chopped into its downed body with sword and axe until the beast was split open from sternum to belly, from shoulder to hip.

Angar leapt past Folkmar and the monster he stood over and into one of the last two giants. The beast swung both fists into Angar's shield and the warrior was thrown to the floor. Angar catapulted from the floor and somersaulted forward with sword at the ready. The jötnar bowed over to meet him and Angar swung his sword into the creature's neck. The blade hit bone and stuck. The beast howled in pain and exploded

68

upward. Angar held to his sword and was lifted off the ground. The monster flailed wildly trying to reach its attacker. Angar held to the sword and lifted his legs and thrust them towards the wall. He kicked off driving the sword through the giant's neck. The jötnar fell to the floor in two pieces. Angar smiled with deep satisfaction.

At the rear of the hall the last of the beasts made its way to the shredded hide. Orn met it head on with a downward swing of his axe. The monster evaded the blow and came at Orn. The jötnar sandwiched its attacker's head between his hands and compressed and Orn's scream was echoed by an explosion of blood and brain matter. Kotkell jumped on the back of the beast and drove his sword through the giant's neck. The giant dropped Orn's headless body and pulled Kotkell from his back and slammed him to the ground. Kotkell's right arm broke and the thighbone of his left leg pierced his skin and pant leg at the impact. Angar rushed forward. He drove his sword through the creature's mid-section then spun around the surprised beast and into the front of it. He jumped onto the giant's chest and drove his dagger into its heart. The beast fell backward and Angar rode it downward driving his dagger into the beast's heart region again and again. Blood pooled from the beast's mouth and Angar punched into its cut flesh and pried its ribs apart. He pried the creature's heart from its body and stood in triumph. He held the heart above his heart and screamed, "I am Agnar Vray, son of Bothvar, son of Einar!"

The hall exploded into cheers.

They chanted "Angar! Angar! Angar!" in a state of frenzied exaltation as their leader devoured the warm organ in his blood-splattered mouth.

Angar washed the blood from his face with a heavy pull of mead.

He kneeled next to Kotkell's broken form and placed his mug to the young warrior's lips. "Drink my friend. You fought well."

Kotkell nodded in thanks and drank. When Angar stood Rognvald and Gunnar set Kotkell's bones as quickly as they could. Kotkell tried not to grimace but couldn't help himself and screamed in pain as the two men pushed his bones back into place.

"Aye," Gunnar offered. "Putting them back always hurts more than the breaking of them."

"Angar's right my son," Rognvald praised, moving to Kotkell's side. "You fought well. Proved yourself a warrior."

"Then I've graduated from dream boy?" Kotkell stammered in pain to Angar.

Angar drank then said, "Bravery in battle doesn't calm a sharp tongue or smart mouth."

"That it doesn't," Folkmar agreed. He faced Kotkell. "I'm living proof of that my one legged friend."

Angar shoved Folkmar in jest then returned to Kotkell, "But it might buy you a pass the next time you outgrow your pants."

Kotkell smiled as best he could and drank heavily from his father's mug.

Angar ordered that drinks be given to all the men and when the task was completed he raised his mug to the air and pronounced, "We are men, all of us. Great warriors!"

The men drank and cheered in agreement.

Angar lifted his mug in the air once more and toasted, "To those who left us this night for Valhalla!"

"To Havard!" Thrain exclaimed.

"To Orn!" Gunnar echoed.

The men agreed with cheers and calls of rejoice and Angar exclaimed, "We will honor them when we do my brother. Havard and Orn will accompany Beigarth into the next life."

The warriors continued their calls and drained their mugs. Thrain and Kol moved from the middle of

72

the hall and filled their mugs once more and returned to fill those of their comrades. Gunnar allowed his mug to be filled then walked among the fallen giants looking them over with heavy interest. He was joined by Folkmar as he stood examining the body decapitated by Angar.

"Ugly bastards," Folkmar commented.

Gunnar pulled his sword and pointed at the creature's groin. Folkmar turned his head in disgust then returned to the pointed area and nodded. These actions were repeated three times more and when completed Gunnar called Angar over.

"Admiring our handiwork?" Angar joked.

"I fear more handiwork will be necessary," Gunnar replied.

Angar responded with a puzzled look. Gunnar pointed with his sword at the beast's sex and said, "Female. All of them."

Angar drank then rubbed his hand along his jaw. "All of them? You're sure?"

"I know gash when I see it," Folkmar declared. "Even jötnar gash."

Angar responded to the joke by calling Hauk to him.

"Deciding what I should do with all these hides I hope?" Hauk offered as he approached.

Angar replied by shaking his head then asked, "The one you skinned, what sex was it?"

Hauk was momentarily shocked by the question but replied, "Male."

Angar cursed under his breath and Gunnar and Folkmar shook their heads.

"What?" Hauk asked.

"These four are all female," Angar declared with anger. "And the one Folkmar killed in the arena was far too small to mate."

"Then there's at least one more out there," Hauk deduced. "A male."

"And far larger than these," Gunnar surmised. "If its species is like any other animal in nature."

"It must be killed," Angar declared. "Its kind wiped from these woods once and for all."

"The colony won't be safe otherwise," Gunnar added.

74

"It will be an honor to fight by your side once more," Hauk admitted.

When Folkmar failed to chime in, the three looked at him in question.

"What?" Folkmar exclaimed. "Now? Or can I finish my drink first?"

*tólf*

Angar and his men removed the giants from the hall and prepared Havard and Orn for burial. Kotkell was sent to recoup in the home of his father and the women of the colony were awoken with instructions to prepare food and to once again clean the Great Hall of signs of carnage. The warriors ate and drank and celebrated their victory until well past dawn. At midday Angar decreed that Folkmar, Gunnar, Thrain, Kol, and Varin would accompany him to "Kill the last of these monstrous animals and wipe their kind from the land."

The men cheered in drunken agreement and in the excitement of the promise of more fighting to be had. Angar reveled in this frenzy for some time before returning to the home of his brother. He entered to find Oubee waiting for him.

"Congratulations on your great victory," the young Beothuk offered handing Angar a mug of mead. "I have prepared a bath for you."

Angar took the mug and downed half of it in one long pull. He put the mug aside and began removing his clothing. "After," he said.

Oubee recognized the look in his eyes and she obeyed by removing her clothes. Her skin was still painted red in celebration of the spring harvest and marked with the tattoos of her people.

She bent over the bed and watched for Angar over her shoulder.

"Not like that," Angar instructed. He made his way to her and put her on her back in the middle of the bed then forced himself inside her. Oubee winced in pain with each thrust. She was suffocated by his size upon her and she pushed against his chest to ease the situation to no avail. She gasped for breath and in her struggle her mind questioned whether this was really happening or if she was in the horror of her dream she'd had the night prior. Angar finished and rose. He drained the rest of his mead and lowered himself into the tub.

"Fetch another mug," Angar commanded. "Then join me."

Oubee rose and attended to Angar's request. She stepped into the bath behind the warrior he directed her to his opposite with his hand.

Oubee did as she was told and lowered herself into the water across from Angar.

"Drink," Angar instructed.

Oubee took a long pull on the mead and returned the vessel to Angar.

"You will lead me and my men into the mountains this evening," Angar instructed. "There is at least one more of the monsters out there."

"How do you…"

"All those we killed were female. There must be a male up there somewhere."

"The Father," Oubee explained.

"The Father?"

"The first Aich-mud-yim," Oubee began. "The first the Maker created. It was he who realized that his kind was made to suffer in the ways of animals. He confronted the Maker…"

"How did the Maker respond to this ungrateful bastard?"

Oubee couldn't help but smile. "He told him to know his place."

"Always good advice," Angar grinned. "Smart your Maker is."

"But I do not know where the Aich-mud-yim..."

"You will take us to where the young one was trapped."

"But, Havard…"

"Havard is dead. Killed in the battle."

Oubee paused before continuing. "But he was the one who trapped the Aich-mud-yim."

"Who helped him?"

"Haki."

"Haki?" Angar asked. "Who is …"

"He was killed on the night the four came."

"Who else?"

"Nonosabasut helped Haki many times. He would know where the young Aich-mud-yim was trapped."

"Nonosabasut?" Angar asked. "He is one of your kind?"

"Yes."

"Good.  Then he will accompany us."

"He does not speak your language."

"Why?"

"He is…How do you say? Vitskertr…"

"Vitskertr? Dimwitted? Soft in the head?"

"Yes, all of these things and more."

"Then it's a good thing you're coming with us."

Oubee took the mug from Angar and drained it.

Nonosabasut led Angar and his party through the
thick forest of spruce and fir northwest of the colony.
When they reached the base of the mountains the young
Beothuk looked to the sun then spoke to Oubee in the
language of their people.  Angar listened to the two and
watched them interact.

"What does he say?"  Angar interrupted.

"He says we should camp here for the night,"
Oubee explained.

"There's still two hours of daylight left," Angar
rebutted.

"He knows this but says the forest above is too
thick and not good for camping."

"Too thick to camp?" Gunnar repeated, joining
in on the conversation.  "That's a crock of horse shit."

"I agree," Angar said.  "Ask him the real reason
he wants to camp here rather than push on."

Oubee spoke with Nonosabasut for several
minutes before turning to Angar in explanation.

"He says it is better to camp in the open," Oubee began anew. "And that it is not good to rush to one's own death for the Aich-mud-yim will surely kill us all for what you have done."

Folkmar laughed, "Nothing like being led into battle by someone with such a positive outlook."

Angar dismissed Folkmar's observation and instructed Oubee, "Tell him we are the greatest warriors on both sides of the ocean and that we will keep him safe so long as he guides us true."

Oubee conversed with Nonosabasut once more. "He said that we will continue for another hour or so until we come to a suitable clearing to camp."

"By the sour look on his face I gather he said more than just that," Gunnar observed.

Oubee lowered her head. Angar lifted it with a finger under her chin. "What more did he say?"

"He said Aich-mud-yim will kill us all," Oubee confessed. "Even those that think so highly of themselves."

Folkmar burst into laughter and slapped Nonosabasut on the shoulders. "Hilarious little imp, isn't he? Honest. Funny."

Angar scowled and directed the guide to continue with a gesture of his hand.

Nonosabasut led the group upward and toward the next rise. Oubee watched with heavy remorse as the signs of the colony's timber industry became more and more apparent. Where there was once impenetrable stands of trees now stood a landscape dotted with stumps and felled tangles of limbs covered in moss and left to rot. Where there was once grass and short shrubs was now an empty channel left to carry soil down the mountain in periods of rain. Oubee recalled picking berries in this same area when she was a child and had she not had the memory of such she doubted that she would ever believe the area could support such vegetation. This clear-cut area gave way to thicker forest much like that surrounding the colony immediate.

The late afternoon sun all but disappeared under the canopy of the woods and the group found themselves in an early dusk when Nonosabasut stopped dead in his tracks. He raised his hand for those who followed him to do the same and Angar verified the motion to his men. The young Beothuk eased backward and passed Oubee who was moving forward to meet him. Nonosabasut stopped when he got to Gunnar. He tapped Gunnar's bow and pointed to the trail ahead. Gunnar responded by lifting the weapon from over his shoulder and knocking an arrow. Angar began to pull his sword but ceased when Nonosabasut shook his head in his direction. Angar returned this instruction with a puzzled look then turned to watch as Gunnar eased his way along the trail before the group. The silence of the area gave way to a low growl. Angar ignored Nonosabasut's order and drew his sword. His men followed and the sound of metal sliding over metal was answered with a ferocious roar of anger. The darkness before Gunnar shifted and distorted as a huge bear lunged forward. Gunnar drew back and fired. The arrow sang forward and buried itself to the feathers in the animal's skull. The bear continued forward caught in the momentum of the charge. Gunnar nocked another arrow and drew back just as the beast came to land at

84

his feet. Without skipping a beat he turned to the group and pondered, "Beast for dinner?"

The men broke into laughter and sheathed their swords.

"I'm so famished I could eat the front hindquarters myself," Varin promised.

"You're not famished," Folkmar chided. "Just hung over."

The group laughed once more and closed in on the fallen bear to assist in its field dressing.

Angar moved to Oubee and instructed, "Ask him if it's safe to have a cook fire here or if it will warn the jötnar of our presence."

The two Beothuk conversed and Oubee returned to Angar's query.

"He said it will be fine so long as he is given the honor of eating the heart"

"So long as he has the heart?" Angar questioned. "For what reason is that?"

"None that I know of," Oubee admitted. "I think he just really likes bear heart."

"Vitskertr," Angar stated.

Oubee laughed and replied, "Yes. Soft in the head."

It was dark by the time the bear was fully roasted and the war party all fed on the meat until they could eat no more. Nonosabasut was given the heart and he ate it raw relaying to Oubee that to cook such a gift would be a waste. The fire was stoked again after dinner and all but Thrain and Varin enjoyed its comfort having been assigned the first watch.

"Ask him how far we will travel tomorrow," Angar instructed Oubee.

She did and answered, "He said we have travelled well. We should reach where the young Aich-mud-yim was captured by late afternoon."

Angar nodded for Oubee to continue. "He says an animal as young as that which was caught wouldn't travel far from its home. That his kind must live near to this place. Perhaps in the mountains just above."

"Ask him if he has an idea where that might be," Angar instructed. Oubee did and relayed the answer.

"He says not far from where it was trapped the forest gives way to a steep cliff and that only something like the Aich-mud-yim could climb it. There is his guess."

"Then we will reach this cliff at dawn following tomorrow's," Angar declared. He looked to his men sitting in the fire's glow. "Sleep well, for tomorrow we push hard and the day following we finish what this scourge started."

The men nodded in agreement and made ready to sleep.

Angar and his group rose before dawn and made their way toward the cliff that Nonosabasut spoke of. The rising elevation was grave and the thick forest difficult to navigate. Despite these hindrances, the expedition made good time and by late afternoon had covered almost all the distance Angar had declared they would. They paused to drink at a trickle of a stream and Angar instructed Oubee to ask Nonosabasut for an assessment.

"Nonosabasut says that the cliff face is not far," Oubee relayed.

"Tell him I want to arrive there at dawn and I need his thoughts on where to camp prior," Angar answered.

Oubee and Nonosabasut spoke for some time and with each passing word the guide grew visibly angry.

"What does he argue about?" Angar asked.

"He says there is no safe place to camp, that the Aich-mud-yim surely know of our presence."

"I'm sure the beast…"

"Nonosabasut says that there are most certainly more than one and that…" Oubee paused. "I think he is afraid. He said he hoped eating the bear's heart last night would give him courage or …"

"Or what?" Angar bid Oubee continue.

"Or that it would make him so dumb as not to care that we rush to our death. He says he prayed that the Maker for one or the other…"

"Are all of your people such pussies?" Folkmar pondered aloud.

Angar fumed, "Tell him he is free to leave prior to our attack so long as he gets us to the cliff by dawn."

Oubee relayed the message to Nonosabasut. Gunnar took Angar aside and said, "What if the jötnar isn't at the cliff?"

"I have no intentions of keeping my word on this matter," Angar decreed.

Gunnar nodded and Folkmar chuckled. Angar ignored them both and returned to Oubee. "What does he say?"

"Nonosabasut says that he does not believe you…"

"Told you he was a smart little imp," Folkmar cracked.

"But that he will do as you command," Oubee continued.

"As well he should," Angar offered.

Nonosabasut led the group along trails left by deer and bear. The woods thinned and the air cooled as they climbed further in elevation. Clouds rolled down from the north blanketing the sky in shades of pewter and gray and brought with them a stiff wind. The expedition continued upward until it was too dark to continue and Nonosabasut announced through gesture that they should camp.

"There will be no fire tonight," Angar informed the group. "Gunnar and I will have first watch. Folkmar and Ted second. Thrain and Varin will share the last."

All nodded in agreement to their assigned duties and made ready for the night at hand.

Oubee dreamt of childhood. She was at play with family and friends in her village. The sky was blue and the sun warm upon her face. She watched as play turned into lessons and as she grew into a young woman and how shy she was when she met the man who was to be her husband. Oubee relived the period in which they got to know one another and as they learned of their shared interests in the things that would bind them in marriage. She watched their families come together at a meal of celebration. The families laughed and shared memories and made jokes about all the happiness the future held for them. There was talk of children and grandchildren and of all the joy that comes with such.

The first arrow entered Oubee's father's skull above his right ear. The second pierced her husband-to-be's neck. The arrows that followed weren't as accurate. They rained from the sky in a spindrift that sent women and children running in all directions. The Norse that followed this aerial barrage slayed the old and the slow with axe and sword, with knife and spear. The female and young were taken by brute strength and some were forced to the ground and tied with rope and others thrown down and held there with a foot or a knee to the back. Oubee watched as she herself was driven into the sod by a Norseman's boot. She struggled and felt the rope cinch tight around her neck and the heavy laboring of breath that followed. She felt the Norseman's hand stroking her shoulder and smelled the stench of his breath as leaned over her. She writhed in panic and the rope tightened even more around he neck. The Norseman laughed over her and his guffaws of pleasure turned somehow into calls of her name.

Oubee.

Oubee.

Oubee.

She jolted awake to the sight of Nonosabasut kneeling over her in the dark.

"Oubee wake," he whispered.

Oubee slapped Nonosabasut's hand from her shoulder and rolled over to see Angar still sleeping next to her.

"Do not wake him," Nonosabasut whispered in the language of the Beothuk. "We must leave now!"

"What is it?" Oubee scanned the campsite to see the others still sleeping soundly in the purple light of pre-dawn.

"We must go. Now!" Nonosabasut insisted.

Angar woke and lunged forward to grab the guide. Nonosabasut launched upward and ran into the darkness.

"Stop!" Angar commanded. The camp awoke with the sound of swords being drawn and men rushing to their feet.

"What the...?" Gunnar started.

Angar rushed after Nonosabasut but stopped after a few steps and returned to Oubee. "Why does he flee? Where does he go!"

Oubee stammered, "I don't know...I don't..."

"What did he say?"

"He said we needed to leave...He was frightened...Something must have scared him."

"Where's the watch?" Folkmar questioned aloud.

"Where are they?" Kol echoed.

"Fan out," Angar bellowed. "Find them!"

The men did as instructed and soon Gunnar called out, "Tracks! Here!"

The group surrounded Gunnar and knelt and watched as he ran his hand over the ground in the growing light. "Here," he said again.

"Not much of one," Folkmar offered.

"No," Gunnar agreed. He continued his study of the ground and soon found another track. And then a third. "Here…There's…"

"Two of them," Kol exclaimed.

Gunnar traced his fingers over the gigantic footprint in the compacted earth then said, "These are far deeper than those in the village."

"They're being carried," Angar exclaimed. "The jötnar have Thrain and Varin."

Angar ripped into the darkness following the double set of tracks. The warriors followed in haste and Oubee struggled to keep up. The sun broke from the darkness and the forest slowly warmed in the soft light of the dawn. It made the trail easier to navigate and illuminated the small clearing it led to. Angar was the

94

first to see it and when he did he fought to control the need to vomit. Gunnar came behind him and almost wept, "The Gods have they…"

Thrain's and Varin's decapitated heads set upon two narrow limbs smashed into the earth. The men's eyes were open and ants and flies were feeding upon these and on the sheared bottoms of their neck. The muck below the crude pikes was soaked in congealing blood and the air surrounding smelled of iron and offal. Oubee came behind the others and put her hand to her mouth in shock. Rage tore across Angar's face and his knuckles turned white in the tight grip of his sword. Gunnar circled the heads studying the ground for sign. He knelt and said, "The tracks lead toward the cliff. Still deep…They're carrying what's left of…"

"Of our brothers," Angar exclaimed.

The forest reverberated in twin roars so loud and deep they seemed to echo from the beginning of time. Angar ran in their direction and his men followed. Gunnar held back and pointed to the dagger at Oubee's hip. She pulled it and Gunnar instructed, "Stay close."

The roars continued and the war party bore down on their source with berserker speed and ruthlessness. The trail opened and before them lay two hundred yards of littered rock and stone between them and the cliff. Two giants stood at the base of the monolith bellowing in anger, each waving a limb topped with the skins of Thrain and Varin. Beneath the beasts was a painting of blood and intestines and the hollowed shells of what were once men. Oubee saw the horrid scene as it was and stated such under her breath. "They did as you did to them."

Kol was the first to charge and he was followed by Angar and Folkmar. Gunnar put his arm in front of Oubee to stop her and launched three arrows before his kin had covered half the distance to the cliff. The larger of the beasts took all three arrows to the chest and it howled in pain and dropped the staff holding Varin's flayed skin. It took the limb back in its hand and ran to meet Kol head on. Kol swung his sword to block the staff and the wood was dissected in two. The giant continued forward and drove its gripped piece of limb through the warrior's chest. The beast followed through and drove Kol's body to the ground and staked him to it. The giant rose in triumph and two of Gunnar's arrows pierced its neck. The beast grabbed its throat in shock and fell dead over Kol's form.

The second giant broke its pike over its knee and made ready for Folkmar and Angar. Folkmar attacked first and the beast met the Norseman's blade with the limb in its right hand. The wood splintered and the monster swung the other log into Folkmar's already wounded ribs and sent him to the ground lurching in pain and gasping for breath. Angar cut wide and his sword opened a foot long gash three inches deep across the beast's abdomen. The giant howled and brought its wood down on Angar. Angar blocked it with his sword but the momentum of the goliath's downward blow sent him to the ground. The beast reared back and came down at Angar with both fists. Angar thrust his sword up and through the monster's left hand. The giant screamed in agony and reared back again but not before Angar turned the blade taking off three of its fingers. Angar pulled his sword and rolled over and onto his feet. The monster hit Angar in the chest with its mangled fist and the Norseman flew backward and into Folkmar. The dying warrior passed his sword to Angar on cough of blood and attempted to say something but was unable. Angar leapt to his feet with a sword in each hand to see the blood soaked beast run towards the cliff. The giant leapt onto a boulder at the base of the precipice, screamed then disappeared behind the huge stone. Angar charged the cliff and vaulted atop the boulder. He dropped down between the rock and the cliff. A blood trail led him along the rock face to a tall split in the granite. He stepped into the cleft just as the call of "Wait!" bounced about its walls. He turned to see Gunnar standing atop the boulder. Gunnar dropped to the ground and repeated, "Wait!"

"For what?" Angar fumed.

"Gods know what's in there…"

"I know of only one way to find out."

"Then we'll go together…"

Gunnar paused mid-sentenced at a sound above and behind. He turned, "Oubee! I told you to stay with Folkmar."

"There is no need to do so," she said.

Angar ran his twin blades over one another in a sharpening motion. His face tightened in rage and the steel muscles of his neck and shoulders throbbed. Gunnar dropped his bow and pulled both sword and axe and gestured forward with his chin. "After you."

The narrow vein into the mountain soon
widened and Angar and Gunnar found themselves at
the mouth of a rock wall chamber three to four times
the size of the Great Hall. Beams of light shown
through clefts in the cathedral ceiling and it took a
moment for the warriors' eyes to adjust to a gloomy
darkness dissected by intermittent rays of narrow light.
The first thing to come into view was a ground littered
with the remains of animals, torn pieces of hide, broken
bone, dried offal, and intestine withered into twisted
strands of leather. The floor also held piles of broken
saplings, furrows of leaves and pine needles and grass.
The air was heavy with the smell of death, putrid meat,
urine, and both fresh and rotting vegetation. It was a
den of unimaginable evil and Gunnar questioned how
such a place could even exist.

"How could the Gods allow…"

"There," Angar interrupted and pointed across
the cavern. "There he is."

All that was visible in the gloom at that distance was the beast's shoulders and back. Its dark pelage was salted with gray and silver and crisscrossed in raised scars and bald patches. It stood and only then did Gunnar and Angar see that it had been kneeling over something. Angar recognized the frame lying upon the ground by its blood soaked arm and butchered hand. The one that stood turned to reveal a chest more scarred than its back.

"The male for certain," Angar decreed.

"Near to six *ell* in height," Gunnar stated in disbelief.

"Seven," Angar corrected.

The giant stood four heads taller than the one on the ground and almost twice as broad. Its face was a history in violence and past fights and its left eye was the color of milk and bisected by cicatrix. The monster turned its head to view Angar and Gunnar with its good eye and flared its nostrils to better smell the intruders. It breathed in the warriors scent then thrust its chest forward and roared with such force it shook the mountain. Angar screamed in response and raised both his swords. Gunnar raised sword and axe and asked, "From the front?"

"No! He's mine alone," Angar spit. "Just be certain the other is dead."

"With pleasure," Gunnar answered.

Angar bellowed in rage and sped forward. The giant roared in response and rushed to meet him.

Angar vaulted through the air with both swords pointing forward and towards the giant's chest. The giant cocked back and swung into Angar. The Norseman's left sword pierced through the giant's right hand. The connecting blow sent Angar across the cavern and into the wall. Angar cried in pain and fell to the cavern floor and grasped his shoulder. It was dislocated. He forced himself up and smashed his body into the wall, thrusting his shoulder back into place.

At the rear of the cavern, Gunnar straddled the dying beast's chest. The fallen giant growled in pain and fear. Gunnar grinned in vengeance and drove his sword into and through its heart. The beast cried one last time and Gunnar stood to pull his sword free. The male turned, pulled the sword from its hand and tossed it aside. It grasped Gunnar in his hands and squeezed. Gunnar moaned in pain and drove his axe into the beast's left wrist. The giant yelped in agony then angrily lifted Gunnar over his head. He drove Gunnar down and onto the sword still lodged in its mate's body. Gunnar's chest burst outward as the sword's grip pierced his body. Angar made it to his feet just in time to see his kin dissected in two as the great giant pulled Gunnar's body lengthwise from his sword.

All of the hatred, anger, loss, bravado, and fear within Angar spewed forth on a cry that rivaled that of the male giant's in volume. Blinded by rage, he gripped his remaining sword in both hands and drove towards the beast. The giant beat its chest in acceptance and ran to meet his challenger. Angar unleashed a barrage of swings and each came with the fury of those he had lost.

"For Beigarth!"

"Asta!"

"Haki!"

The beast flailed its arms in protection to no avail. Angar's blade cut through flesh and painted the walls with slung blood.

"For Havard!"

"Thrain!"

"Varin!"

The giant fell to its knees and Angar charged closer, slicing into and through the jötnar's chest in frenzied strokes from left to right, right to left.

"For Kol!"

"Folkmar!"

Angar sliced through the giant's windpipe and its head bobbled on a torrent arterial of blood.

"For Gunnar!"

The Norseman drove his sword into the already dead Goliath's eye. The behemoth fell backward and Angar rode its body to the ground. The Norse warrior fell to his knees upon the beast's chest and drove his sword to the hilt into the last of its kind's brain through its eye. With the last of his breath, he commanded, "I am Agnar Vray, son of Bothvar, son of Einar!"

He leaned on his sword for support.

"Sagas of my skills in battle are told round fires and in halls on all known lands…"

In his struggle to catch his breath, Angar failed to hear Oubee ease behind him. His peripheral vision didn't catch her hand jut toward him. And given the sharpness of the blade and the speed of the action he didn't feel his neck open until it was too late. He cupped his throat to stave the blood but knew from the feel of the wound there was no need. He fell forward and rolled over to see the Beothuk one last time. She sheathed her dagger and smiled at Angar's forced last words.

"With spear, axe, and sword I have no equal…and though I lie dying on the field of battle, I prepare to enter Valhalla having never been bested in combat…By man."

# About the Author

Gayne C. Young is the best selling author of *Teddy Roosevelt: Sasquatch Hunter, And Monkeys Threw Crap At Me: Adventures In Hunting, Fishing, And Writing*, the Editor of *Game Trails Online*, the official online magazine of the Dallas Safari Club, and a columnist for and feature contributor to *Outdoor Life* and *Sporting Classics* magazines. His work has appeared in magazines such as *Shooting Sportsman, Petersen's Hunting, Texas Sporting Journal, Sports Afield, Gray's Sporting Journal, Under Wild Skies, Hunter's Horn, Spearfishing*, and many others. His screenplay, *Eaters Of Men* was optioned in 2010 by the Academy Award winning production company of Kopelson Entertainment. In January 2011, Gayne C. Young became the first American outdoor writer to interview Russian Prime Minister, and former Russian President, Vladimir Putin.

Again, I greatly appreciate you taking the time to read my work.

Please consider leaving a review wherever you bought the book or telling your friends about my book to help spread the word.

Please visit me at my website www.gaynecyoung.com.

CPSIA information can be obtained
at www.ICGtesting.com
Printed in the USA
FSHW010607261218
54693FS

9 781508 906391